The Adventures of

JACK STACK

The Early Years

The Adventures of

JACK STACK

The Early Years

BOB LAW

Triple Fox Publications, LLC

Dedication

To both young and
young at heart

Dear Reader

This is the story about Jack Stack, a young adolescent boy growing up in the 1950's and 1960's. Jack had a lot of challenges, and in the pages of this book, he tells you about the early years of his life. In each story you may find a way to relate to a situation in your own life, and possibly come up with a solution you may have not thought of before.

Perhaps you can put yourself in his shoes, feel what his life was like, and conclude that your life is not so bad after all. On the other-hand, as and older reader, you may find yourself reminiscing about times in your own life. In either case, you're sure to enjoy these short adventure stories.

More books will follow where I share later years, and more experiences in the life of Jack Stack.

Bob Law

Chapter One

DON'T COME BACK!

"**D**ON'T COME BACK!"

My stepfather's anger still echoes in my ears; his voice embedded in my mind, as I boarded the Greyhound bus for my twice-a-year visit with my biological father.

"You're an anchor holding us down, so don't come back!"

I turned around. "I love you, Mom. I'll be back."

Mom wasn't much for words, but I could see the hurt in her eyes. This was repeated twice a year.

I got on a Greyhound bus fifty-five minutes after midnight in Orlando, Florida, bound for Baltimore, Maryland.

What an education for a boy of thirteen.

My childhood was normal, I guess, whatever normal is. My earliest memories are when I was around five. We lived on a dead-end street (the French call it a cul-de-sac) with only seven houses.

Our house was cedar shake with a big front porch and a white picket fence. I rode my little tricycle up and down the walkway and played on the front porch.

I remember sitting out there with my mother. We loved watching the thunderstorms from the comfort of that porch. I was fascinated with the weather, the lightning, rain, all of it.

When the thunder would roll, Mom would say, "God must be bowling."

Little did I know how important weather observation would be to me for the future.

My sister Edie was nine years older than me and was my babysitter. We really got along well, and I looked up to her. She taught me as much about life as you could teach a five-year-old.

Close to the road, there was a bushy tree in our front yard near the fence. Edie and her friends would hang out there as it gave them a little privacy.

Once my dad caught them smoking behind the tree, so he cut it down.

So much for that.

During the day when Edie was in school, I would play in the front yard and ride my trike and such. Back then, a milkman delivered milk to people's doorstep. I remember our milkman, Harry, from Cloverland Dairies. He used to bring me little trucks that were painted just like the big one he drove. Mom fixed him breakfast while I played with my new truck outside on the porch.

I was the only young boy on our street, but there were girls my age who lived in the houses on either side of ours.

In kindergarten, we played together and went to the same school at the end of the street. Sometimes we would *break out* and go to my house. The basement window was always left unlocked, so we used to sneak in.

Well, we finally got caught and found that was not such a good idea. I guess the people at the day care went crazy looking for us.

Our dad used a common way of those days to discipline us, a switch from a weeping willow tree out back. He could strip all those buds off with one quick swoop. My sister and I got our share of *correction* from that tree.

One time my sister put a small frying pan in her pants, and when Dad found it, she really got a whipping. An interesting twist (or on the flip side), when our pets died, we buried them under that tree. I have a lot of good and bad memories of that tree.

My parents argued a lot. Mom and Dad both worked, and that took a lot of time away from us kids. It seemed they argued most of the time, and the stress level at home was high.

We were told the reason Dad had two jobs was to *make ends meet,* but I didn't understand what that meant. I would later on, of course.

When Edie was fifteen, she married her high school bus driver just to get out of the house.

Me? I just lived life as it came until my parents got a divorce. Then Mom and I moved away from my friends and the suburbs.

Things started to change; now I was a Baltimore city kid. I made new friends, and I learned to roller skate. I'd strap on the skates and be gone most of the day exploring the Big City.

One of the fun things we used to do was put a penny on the streetcar tracks and wait till one came by, and then we would find the penny all flattened. We would laugh and do it all over again till we ran out of money.

Didn't take much to keep us entertained.

When I was about ten years old, Mom moved in with a guy she still worked with, and for the first time, there was alcohol in our house. I wasn't used to the parties and the drinking. I felt a little scared around them when they would drink. Maryland crab cakes, a seafood favorite, and beer began to be a normal thing.

The row houses in the city had marble steps out front that the women scrubbed and kept bright white. They sure were pretty when the sun hit them just right. The back yards were small, and each had an alley, which ran the full length of the block behind the small yards. The alleys ran parallel to the roads on each side of the block, so it made for a quick shortcut when you were being chased.

I started to just lose interest in school, so my grades weren't the best. I could walk every day to the PS-99 public school, just up the street. I found out the PS stood for public school, and the 99 was the ninety-ninth school in Baltimore.

There were kids of different ethnicities in my classes; this was my first exposure to integration, although, we didn't call it that. We were all just kids. One of my best friends was a kid of a different color. We didn't notice, and we didn't know of such things. We all played ball, skated, and explored the city together. The color of our skin didn't matter.

We used to go to Patterson Park to watch the baseball and softball games. Once in a while, someone would break a bat and give it to us. We would take the bat home, wrap it with tape, and have our own game. If we didn't have a ball, we would wrap a roll of electric tape around an object until it was big enough to hit with the bat. We had to be resourceful.

In the winter, the heat in most all of the row houses was steam heat. That meant we had a radiator in each room where the steam from a boiler in the basement would circulate and heat the room. Not very efficient, but it kept us warm. I remember Mom putting a pot of water on the top of the radiator to keep warm for coffee or tea. It also had another purpose, it added humidity to the air.

The city kept the streets cleared of snow in the winter, so we were still able to skate around the neighborhood. When I had kids of my own, and we went to a roller rink, they were amazed at my skating ability. I could hear them saying, "Hey, look at Dad, not bad."

Little did they know that, out of necessity, it was my mode of transportation when I was their age.

When I was in my teens, we finally moved from the inner city into a real house in a suburb called Parkville. I had my own room on the second floor and thought I was king. Well, another school, new friends, and now my very own bicycle to get around on.

Parkville was a small town, only about five blocks long, but it had lots of little stores to explore. There was a Woolworths Five & Ten Cent, an Army Navy Surplus, a bank, and a bowling alley. There were other stores, but they didn't interest me at the time.

The surplus store was a great place with all kinds of things a young boy could use for exploring outdoors. I used to go into the store, look at all the old army stuff, and dream of camping; but I never did go camping until I was an adult.

The Boy Scouts from around the area would get some of their supplies there, but I would just walk around and look and look and look. I didn't have any money, so that's all I could do.

When Owens boat dealer was closed, I would climb up on the cruisers, and using my imagination, I would pretend to be out on the water. I vowed that when I grew up, I would buy my own cruiser and sail the oceans blue. I never did get a cruiser, but I did buy a sailboat, and I cruised the Saint Johns River in Florida.

Upstairs of the bowling alley was a bingo hall. My mom and stepdad would go every Friday night and play bingo for hours and hours. It was pretty boring for me; I hated that smoke-filled place and would go outside to get away from it.

Parkville was just outside the Baltimore city limits where there was a bus and streetcar turnaround. If you needed to go into the inner city, this was how you traveled. Occasionally, I went to visit my sister who lived on the other side of town. It took about an hour and a half one way with transfers and delays, and I traveled alone. I had to change buses in deep downtown where all the low life lived. That was another education. Not necessarily pleasant, but interesting. For example, Baltimore's Block, I was approached a couple of times.

Chapter Two

THE BUS RIDE

THE GREYHOUND BUS would leave the Orlando, Florida bus station at 12:55 a.m. I always had a good seat because, being a thirteen-year-old boy, the bus driver would make me sit up front, so he could keep watch on me. It offered some sort of protection from the characters who sat behind me.

I rode all the way to Washington, DC, without changing buses, so I kept the same seat most of the way. One time I sat in the middle of the bus, and what an education I got, just listening. There were conversations of finance, family, marriage, and divorce, and yes—sex.

I remember vividly watching out the window, the bus rolled back and pulled out of the station into the night. It first passed over Lake Ivanhoe with the Orlando lights reflecting on the water. The lights shimmered only a little bit as the nights were calm. Sometimes, I could see the reflection of the moon, what a wonderful sight.

Not too long after, we would cross over the St. Johns River bridge, east of Sanford. I would think of all the snook that were caught out of the river and wished I would have caught one of them. They are beautiful fish with a black line going down the middle from gills to tail. Most snook are at least two feet long (it seemed to me), and they gave a good fight.

There was a power plant on the river with four lighted red and white smokestacks. I'm sure someone could use them as a landmark, I know I did.

The rest of the night was usually pretty much a blur as we traveled through a lot of dark open country. I closed my eyes and dosed off and pretty much missed what we were passing. The bus would stop at an occasional small town with a service station to pick someone up or drop them off. I would wake up, but then I'd fall back to sleep.

The first time I saw the sun come up was on one of these bus rides. A lover of sleep, I seemed to miss them unless my mom and stepdad woke me up for a sunrise Easter service. I was not interested and promptly went back to sleep while they watched the sun come up over a lake.

Because of the early hour, those services of any kind never did get me excited.

The bus would stop for lunch or a twenty-minute rest break. I had to really keep an eye on my Timex wristwatch, so I wouldn't miss the bus. Now in my later years, and looking back, I realize the driver would not have left me. But these stops taught me how to manage my time, for fear of being left. I also had to manage my money, so it lasted for the whole trip. These would be valuable lessons for me in the future.

During the daylight hours, I had the chance to see a lot of country. There were no Interstates, only country roads and highways, so life was up close. In the south, I would see lots of small houses set back in the trees with people sitting on the porches in rocking chairs just watching the traffic go by cooling themselves with homemade hand fans.

I always wondered if they could hear the bus coming and yell, "Here comes another one!" so they could run to the porch and watch. It didn't take much to keep some people happy.

I saw a lot of people walking down the roads where there were no towns for miles. I wondered where they were going. There were young girls and boys and folks dressed in coveralls; I assumed they were going to work on a farm somewhere. There surely were no stores or factories around.

Have you ever noticed that when you cross a county or state line, there is always a bump in the road? I did. I learned that's not the dividing line between states or counties. That's where one minimum paving bidder stopped and another one started. Our roads are built by the lowest bid. I guess that's why they are continuously working on them.

Interesting.

I fell in love with the trees, the road, and the adventure. I was always amazed at what lay down the road, and around the curve. The roads and the train tracks had bridges to cross rivers that ran parallel with each other. There were long bridges and little, short ones.

There were big houses, and small houses, and some in a row that all looked alike. It was all a great big adventure for a young boy traveling alone in his early teens. I've often thought that's why I don't mind the driving part of the *road trip* today. Truth be told, I'd rather drive than fly.

The larger cities didn't interest me. For the most part, they were dirty, crowded, and people generally had a bad attitude, and no one seemed to greet each other when they passed on the street. A big town preference to me is population 478, and that's just fine.

In the south, people in town would greet each other by saying, "Hey" to which the other person would reply back with another "Hey." In the northern towns if you said that, they would jump back like they thought you were going to do something to them. It was interesting, the culture change between the north and the south. When we would roll into a new town, I would watch the people and observe situations. (That's another book in itself.)

One of the most interesting stops was in Washington, DC. I had a four-hour layover before the next bus to Baltimore. It was a seedy town even in the sixties. There were people dressed in all sorts of fashions, and some didn't have much on at all. Later, I would find out the scantily dressed were prostitutes and people of ill repute. There were *pick pockets* all around, and yes, there were policemen on duty. The thieves would distract you, so they could pull something of value from your pocket or take your wallet.

Sometimes they worked in pairs—one to distract and the other to take from you.

Several times, I was approached by older men and sometimes older women and asked to do them favors like, "Would you go and get me a candy bar young man, and I'll buy you one, too." I was coached by my adopted daddy about such things and never gave in because I knew when I came back, all my stuff would be gone.

There was one man who saw my guitar case and wanted me to play him some songs; he said he had an apartment close by… Boy, I saw that one coming and said "No, I'm just sitting here till my bus comes." He was persistent and said many times, "You're a good boy, I like you." Before long a police officer came by and told him to leave; was I glad! There were a lot of people up to no good.

The Baltimore bus finally came, and in about an hour, my dad met me at the Baltimore bus station. I was really glad to be home and able to get a good night's sleep.

I had to do this trip twice a year, one month every summer and every other Christmas and Easter. The trip back was just as interesting with additional educational opportunities. It was a fun but scary part of my life that taught me a lot about people and travel. Would I do it again? Maybe not, but I'm always up for a road trip!

Chapter Three

FISHIN'

I'VE BEEN FISHING for as long as I can remember. When I was five years old, I would go with my dad and take my little cane pole to catch some sunfish. We went to a place called Gunpowder Falls and fished in the stream below the dam. It was exciting pushing that little worm on the hook and tossing it into the stream. The little bobber would take a dive, and Dad would say, "Now! pull now!" and sure enough, I had caught a little fish. It was too small to keep, but it looked big to me.

Later that day, after we had stopped fishing, Dad would take me up on the observation platform to feed the fish in the deep water above the dam. Wow, we should have been fishing up there, but I guess it was off limits.

These trips always ended with a stop for a big cone at the ice cream store.

Mom and Dad were not on good terms, and when they would argue, Dad and I would go fishing. Sometimes, we would fish two or three times a week. There was times Dad just waxed his car while I fished. I guess waxing helps relieve stress.

Later, I got a real fishing rod, and I learned to cast. Now we could get bigger fish; big enough to eat. We rented a boat and could go farther out into the lake above the dam. That was more fun and a different view than from the shore. Sometimes, we would troll along the shore looking for that big one lurking in the shallows waiting for lunch to swim by, but we never found one. I learned that fishing is more than catching fish, it's about learning to relax and think.

Occasionally, we would try our hand at trout fishing in a stream. After a long drive, we would pull over and make our way down a hill to a stream, usually next to a railroad track. This is where I first encountered real live hobos living along the tracks. Dad would tell me, "Just keep on walking and don't say anything."

Later on in life, I learned they were just people, and each had a story. Nowadays we call them *homeless.*

When Mom and Dad divorced, I moved to Florida with my mom. Florida fishing was different but opened a whole new era of the sport for me. Now I was catching largemouth bass instead of little sunfish.

The first place we stayed was in a rented mobile home behind a motel in Orlando. There was a large lake behind us, and the owner of the motel took a likin' to me. He took me out on the lake in his pontoon boat. He taught me how to drive the boat and let me take some of the motel guests out to fish or just take a little cruise. Not bad for an eleven-year-old boy! Sometimes I would get tips. I would go fishing after school and on the weekends; it was a good time. We moved around quite a bit, but I always came back to that lake.

As we moved from place to place, it was common to see me, headed out to one of the local lakes around Orlando, with my fishing rod strapped to the back of my bike like a trailing antenna. Occasionally, I would stop on a bridge where people were fishing *off the bridge.*

Most of the time the water was murky or brownish color, but sometimes it was clear as a pane of glass, and I could see all the way to the bottom of the lake. I could also see alligators. They didn't have those back home.

On one occasion, at one of those bridges, I met my adopted daddy, Cliff. That's one who you look to when you don't have a father at home, or one you don't respect. More about that in another chapter.

Cliff and I talked for a long time, and after the people left, he asked if I wanted to fish in the judge's private lake.

A judge? A private lake? Sure.

This man worked for a retired judge as a grovekeeper who had a cabin on the lake. We could fish right off his front porch. I caught several crappies. He taught me how to dress them, and how to cook them. Man, were they good.

I rode home and took some with me to show my mom how to cook them—was she surprised!

Next day, I went back to see Cliff, and he took me out on the lake in a boat. This was nice because it was calm and sheltered. Before too long, I got a bite, and it seemed to be fighting more than any other fish. When I reeled it in, it was a four-pound largemouth bass. Woo wee, was I excited! This was the biggest fish I had ever caught. I was so excited, I couldn't wait to start again.

I gave another cast and got a hit; it felt bigger than the first. I reeled it in again but must have pulled too hard because my line broke. I lost the fish *and* my three-dollar fishing lure. I told Cliff we had to show my mom, so I could get another lure just like the one I lost.

When we drove back to my house, I introduced Cliff to my mother and took a picture of my fish. Cliff and Mom seemed to hit it off, so she never had any issues with me going to his place to fish. After all, it was a private lake.

Chapter Four

MY ADOPTED DADDY

AFTER MOM AND DAD got a divorce, I lived with my mother and the other man in her life. We lived in close proximity of my dad, and the courts decided to have me spend every other weekend with my dad, which I did. It was really confusing to me as I would go to my dad's Baptist church on his weekend and a Lutheran church with my mom on hers. Even though I was confused, it was interesting.

My dad and I would go places and do a variety of things. This is where I learned to window shop and found so many interesting things. Often, we would also do a lot of fishing and hunting.

Mom and her new man wanted to move to Florida and take me with them, but they had to get permission from the courts. The court wouldn't let them take me unless they were married, so they got married. Next, as a young ten or twelve-year-old, I was put on the witness stand in court and asked to choose who I wanted to live with. That was one of the toughest decisions I ever had to make. I remember sitting on the stand and looking at my mom and then looking at my dad and back again. I loved them both and didn't want to hurt either one. I remember crying and saying, "I'll stay with my mother."

My dad cried as well, and that hurt me. It was a hard decision. Even the physical and mental abuse from my now stepfather didn't seem as big to me as my love for my mother, or her love for me.

Well, plans were made and off we went in a 1957 Chevy to Orlando, Florida. They chose Orlando because the parents of the other man, now my stepfather, had retired to that city and told them how nice it was.

I wasn't impressed.

The mental and physical abuse continued. One day, I was shining up my bicycle, and my stepfather said, "Why don't you ride that thing instead of always polishing it?" That was it. I grabbed my fishing rod, got on my bike, and rode away. I was so angry. I didn't know how far I rode that day, but later found it was about eight miles. I was looking for a good place to go fishing, as that was my one big way to relax.

On the way back home, I crossed this little bridge where a man, a woman, and two kids were fishing from the side of the bridge. There was another man there as well, and they were all talking.

The family had to leave and that left this other man and me. We talked about fishing and how clear the water was, and we could see the fish bite the bait.

This is when I met Cliff.

The property the judge owned was next to the bridge we were fishing from. We walked down the judge's driveway to Cliff's front porch where we caught a few fish, but it was getting late, so I left and went home.

Cliff became a good friend to me and my mother. We had him over for dinner and game night several times. Yahtzee was one of our favorite games to play while Mom cooked stuffed bell peppers. It was all a good fun night. Sometimes it went on for hours and hours with Cliff, my mother, and my stepdad.

On Sundays, Cliff and I would go to various small churches and attend what was called a *sing*.

We would go to the service in the morning and sing gospel songs till about six o'clock in the evening.

Cliff was a member of the Orange County Sing Association, and we would go to the ones that served dinner on the grounds; between church and singing, they would have a huge dinner where everyone brought food and spread it on long tables for all to eat. We went for the food and sang as a thanks.

I guess you would call it singing for dinner.

On one of these trips through the country, where there were only orange groves, Cliff stopped the car abruptly, looked over at me, and said, "Get out!"

I looked at him with a surprised look.

What is he doing? Is he putting me out in the middle of nowhere to walk home?

I managed to ask, "What?"

He said it again. "Get out!"

"What for?"

"Get out and get under the wheel of this car and drive."

Whew, was I relieved I didn't have to walk home. I changed seats, and for the first time, I was in the driver's seat in a 1958 Chevrolet Biscayne with a standard transmission with the shifter on the column.

Cliff was very patient with me as I shifted through

the gears and drove for twenty-six miles through acres and acres of orange groves on my first-time driving. There was only one other car on the road coming from the opposite direction, and that was a state trooper. I know I tensed up.

Cliff said, "Just keep driving, don't worry about him."

That was the beginning of my driving adventures.

We drove all over Florida, and I learned lots of new things. Sometimes we would just drive and explore other towns and roads just for the joy of driving and seeing new sights. One time, I pulled into a gas station and chose to pull in on the left side of the pump, which was the wrong side. The hose was draped on the outside of the concrete barrier of the island, and you guessed it, my bumper clipped the hose and cut it like a knife. Good thing there was no pressure on the hose.

Cliff did not get upset. He just directed me to drive on the correct side of the pumps. No damage to the car, and the gas station had another hose. I guess that had happened before.

Cliff became a good friend and became the father figure I looked to for advice and such. He would give me insights on things I thought I would never use, but sure enough, they would come to pass, and I was ready for them.

I helped Cliff a lot around the orange grove. He would weed around the trees and trim them just right.

Irrigation of the grove was interesting. There was an old Ford Model A engine hooked up to a pump down by the lake. We would stretch irrigation pipes up the hills between the rows of trees and start the engine. Water would flow up the hills, and Cliff would move the pipes so that water would run down the hill between the trees. When he thought that row had enough, he would then move the pipe to another row. Water recycled from the lake through the sandy soil back into the lake. Surely ingenious and earth friendly.

On occasion, he would hire migrant workers to pick the oranges during harvest time. That was a lot of fun to experience. They were mostly from the islands, and they would sing and sing all throughout that orange grove. Island music abounded, and I got to experience another culture. Once in a while, one would start preaching to break up the time. All in all, it was a lot of fun.

Cliff also taught me to cook. The first thing I cooked was eggs and bacon, simple, but it got me started. Then I cooked the fish we caught. I learned to make avocado salad from the fruit of two large avocado trees on the property. Boy, that was good!

I never went hungry cause now I knew how to cook and eat my own food. This came in handy later on in life as I experimented with several foods. I even had to teach my wife how to cook some things.

Cliff had an uncanny insight into my thinking. He foresaw an upcoming, potentially bad event in my life. I imagined using my pocketknife on my stepdad.

Things got worse at home with him and me. Each time I would return from the bus trip north to visit my dad, Cliff saw a change in me. He said I looked happier and asked me if I wanted to move back north with my real dad.

"That it would be a good thing."

Cliff said, "The next time they tell you don't come back—tell them okay. Then tell your father all the things that have happened since you moved here."

He told me to pack all the things I wanted to keep because I may not see what was left again. So, the next time I got on the bus, and my stepdad said, "Don't come back," I said, "Okay, I'll stay."

I turned and got on the bus and never looked

THE ADVENTURES OF JACK STACK

back. I was about fifteen years old.

When I arrived in Baltimore, I told my father what had been going on and told him I'd like to stay. He contacted his lawyer who drew up a court document, giving my mom thirty days to reply why she should keep custody of me. If she did not reply, custody would automatically revert to my biological father.

I got a nasty phone call from my mom, and she said they couldn't do that. She never replied.

Now, I'm living with my dad.

Cliff and I would write, and he would tell me how things were going and how happy he was to see me happy. I stayed in communication with Cliff until he died. I am eternally grateful to have had Cliff in my life.

Chapter Five

FOOD

DINNERS GROWING UP were a lot different than they are now. When I was very young, we had a dinner table where the whole family sat around for dinner. There was a specific time when it was ready, and Mom would cook fresh vegetables, breads, and other foods. If you didn't make it for dinnertime—you didn't eat.

I remember we had a big cabinet we called a buffet where Mom kept all the *nice* plates for when we had guests over. I would look at that big ornate cabinet with awe. Adventure was climbing under it and hiding, no one could find me, until I got bigger. We had a separate dining room for the formal dinners when we had guests over.

When Mom and Dad were divorced, my dad and I went to my uncles every other Sunday for dinner. This was an enjoyable time in my life. My aunts and uncle never married, and maybe they enjoyed having a young person around. They all lived in the same house out in the country and had their own chickens, grape arbor, and a garden. We had fresh produce all the time.

My aunts would make their own root beer and sarsaparilla laying the bottles in the sun for several days. I knew not why until later in life, but it was fermenting (good root beer).

One Sunday, the neighbor kid and I were on top of the chicken coup with our sling shots. One of us had the bright idea to shoot at the chickens when one started limping really bad. We both thought something was wrong and quit shooting. I ran to tell my aunt that one of the chickens was sick. She said she would check it out, just go on and play.

My aunts would slave in the kitchen, and I would sometimes watch them cook all day. We would have fried green tomatoes, boiled tomatoes, homemade mashed potatoes, homegrown green beans, yams, and fried chicken.

Later that same Sunday that my friend and I were using our sling shots, for dinner we had country fried chicken.

When I reached for a piece, my aunt said, "Here, this one's for you."

It was the broken leg of the chicken we had shot at.

I guess justice prevailed.

When we moved to Florida, things changed. We no longer ate dinner in the dining room at a special table and time. We started having *TV* dinners and stuff like that, and the times we ate varied.

Boy, I missed being back home.

When I caught fish, we would fry the fish and eat them with hush puppies for dinner. Hush puppies were deep-fried round balls made from corn-meal-based batter.

Sometimes, we would eat at my new grandparents' house, they were my stepdad's parents. My grandmother would cook steak and onions in a cast iron pan. It was good, and I learned how to cook steak that way.

Later, when I moved back with my biological dad, we started going back to my aunts' for Sunday dinners.

I guess you can come back home, at least for dinner.

Chapter Six

JOBS

Moving to Orlando when I was about ten brought new challenges in my life. Now I had to work for the money I wanted to spend. Momma said, "If you want money, you're going to have to work for it."

Selling Christmas cards was one of my first *jobs.* Later, I would try to sell other *products.*

Boy, was that a flop. I found out fast that selling was not for me. I can't count the number of cards, seeds, and candy bars I would end up with and had to eat myself.

An easy job to get here in Florida was yard work. I didn't have a lawn mower, but soon learned how to clear a yard or a lot of brush and tree limbs. I learned a healthy respect for snakes and for different kinds of bugs. Many times, I would move a piece of brush and find a snake underneath. At first, I would just kill them with a shovel or some other tool. Then I would look at it and find out what kind it was. Too often they would be non-poisonous who would keep the rat population down. Only a few times were they poisonous. If they were poisonous, we would keep them separate to sell later; we were very careful, and we never got bit.

South of Orlando, there was a tourist attraction with a snake pit. That was one of my places to earn money. They would buy snakes, to put in the pit, at a rate of fifty cents a foot for non-poisonous and one dollar a foot for poisonous snakes.

Once I learned how to handle snakes, it was an easy way to earn money because there were a lot of snakes around. Non-poisonous snakes have round eyes, and poisonous have cat's eyes with slits as pupils. One time, I caught a three-foot corn snake (non-poisonous) and held it with one hand while I rode my bicycle home.

The looks I got from the neighbors as I rode in were priceless, but I got a dollar and fifty cents.

In high school, I worked for a retired Navy man who owned an ice cream store. This was the first real paying job I got. I was sixteen years old, working at the counter and the walk-up window, selling thirteen different flavors. It was a small store, and the owner made his own ice cream in the back at night after the store closed.

One of my responsibilities was to make the syrup he used for the flavoring. He had a lot of one-gallon jugs that I washed and sanitized. Then I would make the syrup by dissolving a five-pound bag of sugar in the bottle by shaking it after I filled them with hot water.

Boy, that was a lot of sugar.

Then he would add the flavor, and then set it aside to use later. Sometimes, I would prepare ten to fifteen jugs per night. That was fifty to seventy-five pounds of sugar per batch.

One time, he painted the inside of the store and painted over the list of flavors. I had to memorize all the flavors so that when people would ask what flavors we had, I would answer, "Chocolate, vanilla, strawberry, butter pecan, black walnut, maple nut, butterscotch, raspberry, black cherry, cherry, peach, pistachio, and banana."

I learned how to make milk shakes, malts, banana splits, and to cook on a grill. I could curl a big scoop of ice cream with a hollow center, so it looked bigger, without increasing the weight of the scoop, which we weighed from time to time.

I think this is where my work ethic started.

One time, I started doing my homework during a slack time. Harry, the store owner, came up to me and said, "Son, I'm not paying you to do your homework. There is always something to do here in the store. You can wipe the counters down or do something."

That was good advice and was taught in a teaching manner which I appreciated.

We sold a cup of coffee for nine cents. Harry was an old Navy man and said coffee should not be taxed—if we sold it for ten cents, we would have to charge tax. His belief about a good cup of coffee was from his military background, and he stood by that price.

Harry would go down the street for a break from time to time and leave me in charge of the store. He said I was the only sixteen-year-old he could trust with the store, so I guess I passed the test.

As the days drew longer, he would stay longer and longer. I really enjoyed working in this store. Sadly, it is physically gone, but it is still there in my mind. Complications in my family life were rising, and I had to give up my job and move north, but I will never forget Harry Sutherland.

One of the things I wanted to do with my money was to buy a new suit and a good watch. I got a ride into downtown Orlando and found a men's store where I bought a new never-been-worn suit for forty dollars and a new seventeen jewel movement Elgin watch for twenty-five dollars, both of which I had saved and paid for.

My mom and stepdad were furious. They told me I was throwing my money away, and that suit was black, so I must have bought it for my mother's funeral. I didn't even think about things like that.

After that, they decided that whatever I got paid, they would take the biggest part and put it in a box to save for me and give me the rest. If I made forty-three dollars that week, they would keep forty dollars and give me the three dollars to spend. They said I would get it back when I went to visit my dad for the summer.

Summer came, and I asked for a partial sum of money for my trip. Mom sat me down and said they didn't have it and said I could keep my whole paycheck for the trip. I was really upset and vowed to never do anything like that again. I wound up with forty-eight dollars for my trip when I knew there had been over two hundred dollars in the box, and all I wanted was one hundred dollars.

Chapter Seven

PETS

GROWING UP, I had lots of pets, some were just fish, but additionally, I had animals.

When I was very young, about five or six, my sister took me to see the circus in Baltimore. One of the venders was selling little lizards called chameleons. They were fifty cents, but I wanted one. They had tied a string around its neck and a safety pin on the other end of the string. I thought it was really great to have another living thing to care for.

One day, I was in the basement of our house, and the lizard got off of the string and ran away. That was devastating to me, but I got over it.

When I was about seven, my sister got married, and her husband had a pet white rat he kept in a cage. That rat was calm and docile, and I would play with it from time to time.

One day, I took the rat outside and got on my swing to take it for a ride. Our dog, Bing, was tied up outside and was barking and jumping toward the swing but could not get to us because the rope was too short.

Finally, Bing broke the rope, jumped on me, and grabbed the rat by the neck and gave one strong shake. The rat fell on the ground, dead, and Bing walked away as if he had done his job.

I really got in trouble over that.

Later, I got some goldfish. I was not able to play with them, so I lost interest.

They didn't last long.

Next, I got some tropical fish, guppies, and others. I learned to watch and observe as they, too, had a life cycle. When they had babies, they would have to hide in the plants in the fish tank, so the bigger fish didn't eat them.

Another lesson in life.

Then I got a little white mouse and could play with him from time to time. I had a small plastic convertible car that I would put him in and push it around the living room. Once, he jumped out of the car and went under the couch. He was gone for several days, and I would not let anyone sit on the couch for fear of crushing my little friend. He eventually appeared, for food, and I caught him and returned him back to his cage.

I don't know what ever happened to that little creature.

After moving to Florida, I got a rescue dog from the pound. It was what we called a *Heinz 57* variety, meaning it was a mixed breed.

I named her Tricksy as she did a lot of tricks and made me laugh. Tricksy was my best friend. She went with me everywhere and was very protective. I remember her growling at my stepfather on several occasions when he would hit me as some punishment. Sometimes, she would nip at him, which made my stepdad very angry.

Tricksy knew the boundaries of our property, and we could sit on the patio at the back of the house when other dogs would come close to the property line. She would just watch, and when they got close, she would growl a little. All I had to do was to say "Get-um," and she would chase the other dogs off the property. She was a good dog—I still miss her.

After I was married, I had another dog named Mack. He was a Doberman pinscher who was the runt of the litter and had to be taken from the mother before he was fully ready. I would put him in a box at night next to my bed with a ticking clock, to simulate a heartbeat, and an unwashed sock of mine. He would sleep in that box, and every once in a while, he would pop his head up to see if I was still there and go back to sleep for another hour or so.

Mack became a really close friend. I would take him for a walk on the leash, and he would break into a run that I could not keep up with. So, I began to ride my bicycle with him on the leash, and he would pull me all over the place—not much exercise for me, but still a lot of fun, especially when he saw something to chase. Mack was a protector, too. One time, another dog, a chow breed, came after me while we were on the back porch, and Mack dove right in fighting that dog. I came into the middle of it and grabbed the chow by the back of the neck and tail, then heaved that big dog about twenty-five feet off the porch. Mack stayed behind with me, but the chow shook it off and went away.

When we moved into a place that did not allow dogs, I had to get rid of Mack. It was the hardest thing I ever had to do. I gave him to a Doberman rescue, who took good care of him. I cried over this dog when I left him, but I knew he would have a good home.

I didn't have too many other pets when I moved back north, while in my teens, as we didn't have any place to keep them. My biological dad taught that it was cruel to have an animal of any kind if you could not care for them properly.

Good advice.

Chapter Eight

SCHOOL

I NEVER TOOK SCHOOL SERIOUSLY. I considered school as a babysitter, for the most part. It all started with kindergarten. I didn't like nap time, and I don't think a lot of other kids did either. We always seemed to get into trouble with the teachers.

Then, on to the first grade. There was a brick, two-room schoolhouse at the end of the road. I only remember two things about that school, no naps, and the letters of the alphabet around the room. I never thought letters stuck on the wall would be so important, especially learning to write them in cursive.

Elementary school turned out to basically be a no brainer (no pun intended). When we moved to the city, it was still just a school, but I had to walk about eight city blocks to get there, and we had to play in a fenced-in concrete playground. There wasn't much grass in the city, except at the public parks, so we just had to make do.

Junior high school, as we called it back then, was a little better. We had to change classrooms for different subjects, and we were given a locker to put our stuff in. I was still kind of rebellious, but I began to enjoy school.

About this time, my mom and stepdad moved to Florida for another interruption in my schooling. It seemed I had to change schools every six months to a year because my mother and stepfather moved. By the time I finished high school, I could count thirteen or more different schools I'd attended.

Florida schools were different still. The hallways were outside with courtyards in the center. When you had to change classes, you went outside and sometimes to a different building.

Sports was not my thing, but I wanted to join the football team. I was being bullied because of my name, and thought if I joined them, they would stop. Sure enough, I made the team as a half back, and then Mom moved to another district.

In the new school was where I learned to write

stories. The first assignment was to write what you would do if you knew you were going blind in three days. It was called "Three Days To See."

I got an *A* on that, and several more to follow. I guess the success of an *A* was exciting, and I got recognition. Up to this time, I'd always been a *C* student or below.

I had a small typewriter and would write stories in my room. They weren't bad stories, but my mom found one and said, "Who wrote this?"

I said, "I did."

She answered, "No you didn't, you can't write at that age level." She took my stories away.

I then taped a big envelope under the center drawer of my desk and kept them there. I forgot them when I moved away, and she didn't find them for five years. One day when she called, she said, "You can't hide things from me young man."

Well, I did for five years.

Things were going good again, and then I moved back with my biological father.

New school again.

I moved into the school district where my father lived. The school was a big three-story building with an auditorium and a large gymnasium. Major league football players would come play basketball, and singing groups would come for what was called a *Hootenanny.*

There were football fields, baseball fields, and a track to run on. This was the biggest school I'd ever attended. When I enrolled, they had a Creative Writing class, and I thought that would be fun, so I could learn more about writing.

That lasted about two weeks. One of the assignments was to write a descriptive story about someone in the class using lots of adjectives and verbs. Well, there was a girl in the class that also went to our church, and I kind of had a crush on her. So, I wrote a story about her. I imagined I was walking home one night, and as I passed her house, I could see her shadows on the window shade, and I wrote about that, being very descriptive.

The teacher kicked me out of that class saying, "If you're going to write that kind of stuff, you don't need to be in this class."

That was the end of that.

In my senior year, I found out the first absent note of the year was put on file and future excuses were compared to that signature for validation. In the later part of the year, I skipped sixty-nine days, but they were all excused as I wrote the first note of the year.

My senior year found me having girl problems, and my motivation for going to class dwindled.

Sometimes, I would skip school and drive around Baltimore with my uncle. He would take me to the Gayety Burlesque House where I got another education about life.

It seems life is all about education.

Now, my girlfriend dumped me, and I couldn't handle it, so I went down to enlist in the Air Force. Hey, I was eighteen now, and I was too depressed. I needed to get out of town.

The recruiter asked if I had a high school diploma. I told him I was failing this year anyway and just wanted to enlist. The recruiter studied the situation and said he would not take me until I had graduated from high school.

I pleaded with him, and he said, "Look, let's both go see your guidance counselor and see what we can work out."

At the school, we went to the counselor's office and sat down. The recruiter said, "This gentleman wants to enlist, but I won't let him until he graduates. He tells me he is failing. What can we do?"

They looked at my grades and agreed I was failing but said he would have a conference with my teachers and see what could be done. Two days later, each of them gave me a task to do, and if I passed with an *A* on those tasks, they would allow me to graduate. I met with each teacher who gave me a task in their class.   The English teacher's task was to write a thesis on anything I wanted, and if it got an *A,* she would pass me in that class. This was the one I worried about.

I chose to write about the prenatal effects of brain damage on brain damaged children. I had some experience with that concerning a family member.

In addition, I was in the photography club at the YMCA. Each week, I would meet early to go swimming with some of the other members of the club. One member was a pediatric professor at Johns Hopkins University. I told him I was working on a project to graduate and asked him if he could give me a few thoughts. We met for two weeks. As he gave me medical terms and explained them and how doctors made up the words for the terms they used, I took detailed notes and typed up my report with footnotes and all. I turned the paper in and waited.

A few days later, my English teacher asked me to stay after class at the end of the day.

My teacher asked me, "Did you write this?" (*Kind of sounded like my mother.*)

I replied, "Yes."

She looked at me and said, "I'll bet you don't know half of what these words mean."

I said, "Well, ask me a question."

She then pointed to a long medical term, and I gave her the correct pronunciation and the meaning. She pointed to another one and another one, and after a few more, she stopped and said, "Well, I guess you know it."

She then circled one of the footnotes in red as being out of place and marked an *A minus* on it and said, "You passed the class with a *D* average."

I graduated June 12, 1964, and was on the plane to Air Force basic training in Texas, June 17.

I don't recommend this approach.

Chapter Nine

IMAGINATION

YOUR IMAGINATION can run wild if you let it. Sometimes, when you want to imagine, it plays tricks on you.

As a kid growing up in a dysfunctional family, I used to imagine I was somewhere else or being somebody different. It was like playing you're an astronaut or something. You can learn from your imagining things. That's why parents give their kids toys to play with. Hopefully, they will learn to care for others when they give girls dolls and boys fire engines and such.

I was a young man with a big imagination, and I used it quite effectively. As soon as something bad would happen, I'd go into my imagination nation and escape reality for a while. When I felt better, I would return. The problem would still be there, but I felt better about it.

Imagination is where new inventions come from. Tesla, Einstein, Thomas Edison, and others have changed the world because of their imagination. Look what Henry Ford's imagination has done for the automobile industry.

Imagination is where writers get some of their material to write books, movies, plays, and games. Think about *Harry Potter*, *Moby Dick*, *Michael Vey*, the *Adventures of Huckleberry Finn*, and many more. You can change the world, one person at a time, with the books and movies you write using your imagination.

I don't know why, but I used to imagine there were alligators under my bed, and that would keep me in bed as a young child. There were no alligators in Baltimore, and little did I know, I would be associating with alligators when we moved to Florida.

It's funny how thoughts like that come into your mind to prepare you for the future. All we must do is pay attention and listen to that still small voice.

I remember one time the guys I hung with, in Florida, would catch baby alligators and sell them to the tourists. One time, we caught a three-foot gator and kept him in my mother's washing machine for a few days. There was a new family moving into our neighborhood with a big moving van. When the van was empty, we approached the movers for the sale.

"Have your guys ever seen an alligator up close?" I asked.

They all said no, to which I replied, "Want to see one?"

"Sure," they answered.

When we opened the washer, they all looked in, and one man said, "Oh man, that is cool."

Another man said, "Do he bite?"

"Sure, it does. You want to buy him?"

"How much?"

"Five dollars," we said. "How far are you going?"

"We're going back to New York."

We told him it should make it back there okay. (Of course, it was the same answer for anywhere.)

One guy said, "Yes, I'll take him."

So, we took it out of the washer and tied a rope around its neck then handed it to the man who wanted it.

"Oh, no no no!" he said, throwing up his hands.

"Go on, you can lead him around like a dog," we replied.

I told them, "Do you know you can put him to sleep? All you have to do is roll him on his back and rub its belly." Then I showed him. "See."

"Oh, no. You just put him in the back of the truck," he said.

We looked in the now empty fifty-three-foot-long semi and said, "Okay."

We collected our money and closed the door.

Now, here is where the imagination comes into play. A three-foot alligator alone in a semi-trailer for about twenty-four hours. What's he going to do with it when he gets back to New York City? Who is going to get it out? And is he going to get bit, cause now the gator will be mad and hungry.

You also have to imagine what the man who bought it was thinking.

Imagination, it's a wonderful entertainment, and it's free.

My buddy and I would ride our bikes into one of the swamps around Orlando to an abandoned shack. We would climb on the roof and watch the clouds moving and shaping and imagine what we would do if we had a million dollars.

These thoughts took us away to lands and places around the world. I guess this was our beginning of goal setting without calling it that. After about an hour or so, we would climb down, catch another baby gator to sell, and head back home.

Today, those swamps are shopping malls and restaurants with parking lots. I enjoyed these sessions as it helped expand my imagination and dreams. The next step was to put those dreams into actions because imagination without action remains just a dream.

Chapter Ten

BICYCLES

WHEN I GOT my first bike, I thought FREEDOM! Now I could explore and go places.

Back then was a different time, as far as keeping watch on your kids. As long as we were home for dinner, you were good. We didn't have to worry about all the stuff they do nowadays.

My first adventures were around the neighborhood with the girls next-door. We would ride and look at houses, yards, and stuff. They expanded our street to include a new subdivision, and we would explore all the new construction, dirt mounds and all.

My dad did yard work for a doctor, who lived just beyond that new subdivision. We found out where he lived and rode our bikes to see his property. It was nice with a terraced garden and a swimming pool.

While we were looking at the pool, we heard some voices yelling to get away from there. We hightailed it back down the hill and made the turn to get home when we heard some gunshots and bullets striking the trees along the side of the road. Boy, were we scared and counted ourselves lucky we were not shot.

Although, I wondered how they would explain that one if we had gotten hit.

When I got to Florida, the bicycle really came in handy. Places were a lot farther apart. Like a lot of the other kids, I even had the opportunity to ride my bike to school.

I joined up with three other friends from the neighborhood, and we called ourselves The Four Amigos. We looked like a rough bunch and hung out together a lot.

I was glad we moved away from them when I was about fourteen. I found out later that they all had gotten in trouble somehow, and eventually, they all served time in jail.

I would ride my bike for miles looking for new places to fish, and while I was riding, I would sing.

One time, I was singing away, just having a good old time, when a bug flew straight into my mouth.

Talk about shock. My eyes got big, and I started spitting and coughing and spitting again.

I never did get that bug out!

It would have been a sight to see. Thankfully, nobody else was on the road. I always wondered what kind of bug it was, but I still lived, so I guess it was okay.

I rode my bicycle on Interstate 4 in Orlando, before it was opened. It was a good road, and I could ride my English racing bike as fast as I could without any traffic. Today, I-4 is so busy I would get run over if I even thought about it.

My bicycle gave me freedom. Freedom to get away when things got rough at home. Freedom to find new fishing spots. Freedom to explore new roads and open spaces.

Freedom from everyday cares, and most of all, *freedom to be me.*

Chapter Eleven

MUSIC

IN MY EARLY YEARS, maybe eight years old, my parents bought an accordion for me. I think they bought it from a traveling salesman selling the accordion lessons, and a weekly recital which my father had to drive me to in town.

I practiced all week, and then we went to town. There was a room full of kids, mostly girls, and we had to sit to watch the others play before our turn. It was a small hot sweaty room.

The other kids were good, but I struggled. I lost my place several times but kept playing. It was fun, but I was not impressed. Mom and Dad couldn't afford the lessons after a while so that went by the wayside. Door-to-door salesmen would sell anything when I was a kid in the fifties.

I think I was about ten or eleven years of age, before my mom and stepdad moved to Florida, I got a guitar for Christmas. Not a new one, but it was not a kid's guitar.

The neck was warped a little, so I had to press hard on the strings. It used to belong to my stepdad's brother, who drowned one day swimming at the lake. I think they thought I would resurrect his memory or something.

It didn't matter to me; I just had another outlet for energy.

We couldn't afford lessons, so I got a book to teach myself. I would lay in my bed at night trying to remember the chords just strumming until my parents went to bed. I eventually got three chords down, and now I had to put them together.

"The Old Grey Mare" was the first song I played without looking at my fingers. Now I was set.

The first *real* song I learned was "Frankie and Johnny." I learned that one very well, and others from Johnny Cash.

I loved listening to the radio back then and all the old songs of the fifties and sixties. People could hear me singing along with them any time. Some of the other greats I listened to were Ricky Nelson,

Pat Boone, Elvis, and many more. I learned to play "Blue Suede Shoes," and every time some of the parents from church would ask me to sing, I let loose with that one and a couple more of my favorites and even threw in some of Elvis's moves.

They would laugh and giggle between themselves. I wasn't sure if they were laughing at me or not, but I didn't care.

When we moved to Florida, the old guitar was sure to go. It allowed me peace of mind and my own space. I customized it with a red paint job that looked something like Buck Owens on TV.

I would sit with my dog Tricksy on the back patio and strum away. Sometimes Tricksy would sing along.

At least, I had one admirer.

I continued playing for myself until I moved back to Baltimore with my biological dad. I then played a few times in church, but only a few times. I don't think they liked the way I sang some of the hymns.

Oh well, I had a style.

I joined the church choir and had a good time with that. We got to sit in the choir box and wear robes. My girlfriend and I could sit together for a change and hold hands under the robes. Made me feel kind of special.

On occasion, we would change up the beat or rhythm for our special numbers. I had something to do with that, but nobody said anything, so I guess we were clear.

My guitar served me well as I serenaded my girlfriends. Some appreciated it, but I think most just thought, "that was nice," but it didn't bother me much.

Later in life, I played and sang at a pizza parlor with a blind piano player.

That was a sight.

Chapter Twelve

STORMS

WEATHER IS SOMETHING most kids don't think about, but as a young boy, maybe seven or eight, my mother would show me signs of good and bad weather that was on the way.

Such sayings as, "Red sky at night—a sailors delight," meaning the next day was going to be a sunny day. "Red sky in the morning—sailors take warning," meaning the weather would not be good for the rest of the day.

We would watch thunderstorms from our front porch and count the lighting strikes and then count seconds until the thunder sounded. Later in life, I found you could tell how far a storm was away from you by counting. Every six seconds was about one mile, so you could tell if a storm was moving toward you or away from you.

Living up north as a very young boy we had snow in the winter. Sometimes, it would come down so thick you had a hard time seeing, and other times it was so light it looked like a mist.

But most every time it would cover the countryside in a blanket of white, sometimes as thick as a couple of inches, and other times it seemed like a foot or two. In either case, it was cold, and Mom would bundle me up before I went outside.

Mom and I would build a snowman. When we got done, we would go inside and have a cup of hot chocolate. I looked forward to that.

Sometimes, the snow would be very wet and heavy and other times very dry and light. I could never figure out how that happened, but I knew that when it was wet and heavy, the weight would cause the power lines to break, and we would have no power. Then it got cold in the house, and we would have to bundle up, *inside.*

The weather determined a lot of things like how to dress, if there would be school today, or if I needed to stay inside and play, or if I could go outside. When it snowed heavily, Dad and Mom would stay inside and wait the snowstorm out.

Later, after we moved to Florida, we had another set of weather patterns, hurricanes and heavy thunderstorms.

I don't remember the thunderstorms being as strong and intense as when I lived up north.

Hurricanes were another story. We had plenty of warnings that a heavy storm was coming, and people would take extra precautions. They would go to the stores and buy more food and wood to board up the windows and doors. I never understood all that activity until later in life.

I do remember hurricane Donna coming through Florida in 1960. We lived in Orlando, and the storm came within forty miles of our house.

We lived in a single-story house with a sliding glass door that went out onto a patio. The land was pretty flat around there, so the water runoff was not that great. It started raining around four o'clock in the afternoon and got progressively harder and harder throughout the evening.

It really got worse as we got into the night. The wind started blowing harder as the night went on. Rain started coming in around the seams in the windows, and when I looked outside, the water was flooding our patio.

Mom ran and got some towels from the bathroom, rolled them up, and put them on the floor in front of the patio door. The rain kept coming in, and the towels got wet. Mom would take them to the bathroom to wring them out in the bathtub while my stepdad put more towels under the door. This went on for hours, and I helped wring out the towels and put them back under the doors.

The tub started to fill up, and I didn't know what that meant until later. It meant there was no place else for the water to go.

The hurricane lasted most of the night, and about seven o'clock in the morning, the rain slowed down, and we could finally rest. We had bailed water all night.

When the sun came up, I looked outside, and everything was flooded. The whole yard and the streets looked like a lake. There were tree branches and debris all over. Some people had shingles blown off their roof, but others, the roof was completely gone. I had never seen anything like this before.

The power was out as well, so pretty much all we did was sleep and rest. But, with no power, we ate good because we had to use the food in the refrigerator before it went bad. Having a gas stove was a blessing, too, because it still worked.

We had survived our first hurricane.

Mom and stepdad learned to prepare more for the coming storms. Even today, I wonder why the first thing people would store up is toilet paper. I guess it's because they had to eat their own food. (Haha)

Some people say they would never live in a hurricane country. But one good thing, you know ahead of time it's coming, so you usually have days to prepare. You can choose to cither go somewhere else or stay put and prepare for it.

Tornadoes, on the other hand, don't give you a warning. When you see one coming, all you can do is run and hide to protect yourself. If you live in tornado country, just be prepared to lose everything, anytime.

Just my opinion.

Understanding the weather and how it works is a valuable asset in life. It can make your life pleasant or irritating, it's all up to you.

EPILOGUE

OFTEN WONDERED if I was like one of those unruly kids, running around and being rambunctious. Because I grew up in the sixties in a dysfunctional family—and that was not even a definition yet that I knew of.

But it was an interesting journey. I learned about life the hard way but managed to stay out of major trouble. I had adventures and experiences I would not trade anything for as it has molded me into the person I am today.

There was tragedy, hardships, friendships, experiences, people, churches, businesses, jobs, and much more I experienced growing up. I learned about love and being loved, caring for others, and living frugally.

I had a job at a telephone company as an IT person and had an interview for a promotion. When I went for the interview, my boss asked me lots of questions about my job performance.

He then asked, "What kind of certification do you have?" Most people had three or four with the initials behind their name.

I said, "None."

The interview continued:

"You don't have any, not even your Microsoft basic computer?"

"No," I said, "I learned it all on my own."

He then asked, "What are those initials behind your name then?"

As a pilot, I wanted it to look more technical, so I started to put my flying credentials behind my name. CFIA & I MEL means Certified Flight Instructor Airplane, Instrument and Multi Engine.

After much thought, I did have the initials AAGG by my signature.

I looked him straight in the eye and said, "All-Around Good Guy!"

He laughed so hard I thought he would pass out and said, "I ought to hire you just for that."

I didn't get the promotion, but I still use those

initials from time to time. I guess that's what all those experiences have brought me to, and I'm proud to be called an *All-Around Good Guy.*

Life is never as bad as you think it is. Life will always get better—no matter what. When you're sure you are as far down in the dumps as you can go, remember, if you are down to the bottom—*the only way to go is up.*

I wouldn't trade anything for the experiences I've had, they have made me stronger and wiser.

You, too, will be stronger and wiser, just hang in there.

ACKNOWLEGMENTS

I WANT TO THANK my wife and daughters for their support; my writing mentor, Richard Paul Evans, and the Author Ready group, for training, guidance, and encouragement, in getting this book finished.

I wish to thank the United States Air Force for teaching the discipline, and the skills, to make it in this wild and wacky world. Special thanks to J.C. (Cliff) White, for his strong positive influence; he probably saved me from a totally different lifestyle.

I am so grateful for all the things encountered to make this story possible. Many will be used in the development as we walk through the stages of Jack's life.

I am grateful for the opportunity to share Jack's life experiences. I hope others might benefit in some small way.

ABOUT THE AUTHOR

Bᴏʙ Lᴀᴡ has led a unique and interesting life, and he draws on these experiences when creating his stories.

Primarily a non-fiction writer, Bob has been writing since before high school but didn't get serious until his adult years. With an extensive pilot's background, Bob's first book, *My Flying Days Are Not Over,* has seen resounding success in the aviation circles.

Bob is a family man with a wife and two daughters, all successful in their own fields. A respected leader, public speaker, and active in his church and community, Bob has taught personal development classes around the southeastern part of the United States, helping others to improve their lives and be successful in whatever field they choose.

Bob's enjoyable, down-home writing style is intriguing to readers of all ages.

UPCOMING BOOKS

The Adventures of Jack Stack
The Later Years

My Flying Days are Not Over
for Airline Pilots

Watchin' People
Observations of Life

Homeless
How they got that way and how
to keep from going there

May I Help You?
A Caregivers Perspective